In memory of my seafaring dad,
Malcolm MacLachlan, who so
wanted a sailor in the family —C. S.

To my pup —R. R.

BY CAROLINE STUTSON

ILLUSTRATED BY
ROBERT RAYEVSKY

# PIRATE PUP

chronicle books·san francisco

On the window, the first mate was tapping.
He pressed his black nose to the glass.
"Ahoy, Captain Pup. It's time to get up.
The *Rover* is sailing at last, last, last,
The *Rover* is sailing at last."

Pirate Pup pulled on his jacket.

He straightened his patch with a tweak.

"Farewell, Mother dear. Father, don't fear.

I'll return by the end of the week, week, week,

I'll return by the end of the week."

At the harbor, the *Rover* lay ready.
"Heave ho, my Hearties," Pup said.
"It's time to depart. We will get a head start
While the cats are asleep in their beds, beds, beds,
While the cats are asleep in their beds."

From Boston they sped for Nantucket,
Riding the outgoing tide.
Not a worry or care, the weather was fair,
And nary a cat had they spied, spied, spied,
And nary a cat had they spied.

Not far from the coast of Grenada,
In a dinghy, the pirates set forth,
Two dogs at each oar, they rowed for the shore,
Unaware of the cats to the north, north, north,
Unaware of the cats to the north.

"Dig quickly, my Hearties!" Pup ordered.
"X marks the spot. Don't delay.
The map makes it clear. Our treasure is here.
We must hurry and cart it away, 'way, 'way,
We must hurry and cart it away."

By sundown they'd dug up the booty
And stowed it on board, out of sight.
Then they dined on sand dabs, mussels and crabs,
And climbed in their bunks for the night, night, night,
And climbed in their bunks for the night.

Next morning, while hoisting the mainsail,
The crew sniffed the cats near their ship.
"Quiet!" warned Pup. "They mustn't wake up.
Not a sound, and we'll give them the slip, slip, slip,
Not a sound, and we'll give them the slip."

They had sailed past the coast of Barbados,
Feeling clever and wily and free,
When a sailor called out: "Cats ahoy! Turn about!
Let us flit. Let us fly. Let us flee, flee, flee,
Let us flit. Let us fly. Let us flee!"

Too late had they spotted the danger—
Cats boarded the *Rover* with swords.
"We've circled the globe for your treasure of gold.
Your gold or the fishes!" they roared, roared, roared,
"Your gold or the fishes!" they roared.

Down through the galley they battled,
Over barrels and crates in the hold.
From starboard to larboard, backward and forward,
The cats in pursuit of the gold, gold, gold,
The cats in pursuit of the gold.

With new fury, the battle continued,
As the dogs chased the cats to the deck.
"Leave us alone! You shan't have one bone!"
Then the dogs trapped the cats in a net, net, net,
Then the dogs trapped the cats in a net.

"**BONES!**" screamed the cats. "Are they golden?"

"You cannot eat gold," the dogs scoffed.

The cats rolled their eyes. "Dogs!" the cats sighed,

And they jumped to their boat and sailed off, off, **off,**

And they jumped to their boat and sailed off.

2005 bones

The instant the sails had been mended,
The pirates turned north on their own.
With Nantucket in view, they joyfully flew,
Almost home with their treasure of bones, bones, bones,
Almost home with their treasure of bones.

At the harbor, their families waited,
Cheering with tears in their eyes.
"Where have you been?" "What have you seen?"
"Tell us your stories," they cried, cried, cried.
"Tell us your stories," they cried.

Into the Sea Dog all tumbled,

Where they shared their bold deeds as they supped.

While their parents' tails wagged, they boasted and bragged,

And toasted their brave Captain Pup, Pup, Pup,

And toasted their brave Captain Pup.